Blossom's Family Album

By Devra Newberger Speregen

Based on the television series *Blossom*
created by Don Reo.

SCHOLASTIC INC.
New York Toronto London Auckland Sydney

ISBN 0-590-47234-8

Copyright © 1993 by The Walt Disney Company
All rights reserved. Published by Scholastic Inc.

Cover photo: Linda A. Vanoff
Cover design by Elizabeth Parisi
Book design by Dawn Antoniello

12 11 10 9 8 7 6 5 4 3   3 4 5 6 7 8/9

Printed in U.S.A.   08

First Scholastic printing, May 1993

*I*t's like I was telling Six, my best friend: If strangers accidentally found themselves at our house one day, and they had never met any of us — me, Dad, Joey, Anthony, or Buzz — they might think that they had walked into a house from the *Twilight Zone* or something! I told Six it was like we were all part of this big zany television sitcom where odd things happen on a *daily* basis. "Oh, yeah, sure," she said, "just like the Cosbys or the Conners or the Tanners or..." Naturally I had to cut Six off right there because once Six gets started, you have to cut her off or she'll never stop talking. Anyway, the notion of us, the Russos, as America's favorite TV family really cracked us up!

It's funny, with all the unbelievable things that have happened to me over the past couple of years, you would think that by now things would calm down and I could just go on enjoying the normal life of a 16-year-old girl. But it's like my grandfather Buzz always says: "If it's normal, it ain't normal!"

So when my history teacher gave us this assignment — to give a visual report on our home life — at first I was like "yeech," because I had really planned on shopping for clothes at the mall with Six this weekend. But once I started gathering all these great photos and reminiscing and everything, I'm happy that Mr. Kirby gave us this project. I mean, I totally love to write anyway, and this project might turn out to be fun after all. I guess the mall can wait until next weekend!

A visual report on my life? Well, okay. This is me: Blossom Russo, a 16-year-old girl living with her single musician father, one recovering alcoholic brother Anthony, and one ... one ... one Joey. (I am totally lost for words when I try to describe my girl-chasing, slightly dopey brother without insulting him.) My best friend, Six, is a dear sweet girl who talks a zillion miles a minute. I like dancing, writing, singing, and wearing funky clothes and hats.

*T*his is my bedroom. Pretty cool, huh? Dad let me fix it up exactly how I wanted. Most of the stuff I bought at garage sales. Check out all the space I left in the center — lots of room for working out new dance moves with Six.

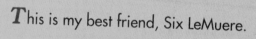
*T*his is my best friend, Six LeMuere.

*T*his is ... *was* my boyfriend, Vinnie Bonitardi. We broke up — again. ... Break up to make up, that's what we do. ... Here's my favorite picture of us. Don't we make a cute couple? I love how I look in his leather jacket.

Six LeMuere

Six LeMuere. Isn't she totally adorable? Our friendship is the best. We've been best friends practically forever, to the point where we can finish each others' sentences. Well, actually, Six usually finishes all my sentences. Come to think of it, she usually starts all my sentences, too!

Although we're the tightest of friends, Six and I have had our share of problems. Like the time we both had a crush on the same guy. Six says that if we can make it through that mess and still remain buddies, we can make it through *anything*! I agree, but sometimes she drives me *crazy* with all the really dumb things she does — like that time she landed us both in jail! But I'll get to that later.

This is Six's mom, Sharon. Last year she and Six's dad got divorced. It was really tough on Six watching her parents split up and all. I felt so bad for her. Since my parents are divorced, I really knew what she was going through so I tried to cheer her up. These days, she's pretty cool about it, though she still secretly wishes they would get back together. I can definitely relate.

Anyway, Six is exactly like her mother. It's really something to watch these two have a conversation. They are both the fastest talkers in the world!

When Six's parents' split, Six spent a lot of time at our house. Some days she didn't go home at all! But I didn't mind — I love having Six around. We can tell each other just about anything.

Vinnie Bonitardi

I met Vinnie Bonitardi at school last year, and even though everybody said we wouldn't last a day, I was *sure* we would!

*D*ad, on the other hand, had a totally different first impression. From the moment he met Vinnie, he knew he wanted him out of my life as much as possible! And things got much worse when Dad caught us kissing on the couch on the night of our first date! Things between Dad and Vinnie really improved, though.

Vinnie and I had some major ups and downs in our relationship, but probably the biggest event was when we ran away from home together. Vinnie wanted to be out on his own and I wanted to be with Vinnie. So when my Dad and I got in this huge nasty fight one night, I sneaked out and split with Vinnie. It was a really dumb thing to do and I ended up coming home the next day. Dad was pretty cool about the whole thing, and very relieved after I told him that Vinnie slept in his car the whole night and I stayed in the hotel room — alone.

Nick Russo

*T*his is my father, Nick Russo. Scary, huh? No, honestly folks — no bunny is cooler than my dad!

*D*ad and I have an excellent relationship. Oh, sure, he can be a real pain sometimes — like when he grounded me for forging his name on my detention slip, or when he almost didn't let me go to the Junior Prom with Bobby. But we've come to understand each other. Dad says we'll get along fine if we follow this simple rule: I don't ask him anything about his girlfriends, and he can ask me anything about my boyfriends. It doesn't sound too fair, but after all, he *is* my father. Who else is going to take care of me and bring me chicken soup when I have a cold?

*D*ad's great with us kids. It must be tough having to raise three teenagers alone, but Dad's doing pretty well. He's always around for us if any of us needs to talk.

Anthony Russo

My older brother Anthony is one of the greatest people I know. He's everything: smart, funny, cute, and very sweet. Anthony has been through a lot in his life, but he's always managed to bounce back. I'm really very proud of him.

A few years ago, Anthony was a totally different person. And not a very good person, I might add. He was addicted to alcohol and he did drugs and it was like we didn't know him. Half the time we didn't know where he was, and I have to tell you *that* was really scary. But for over two years now, Anthony has been sober and he's become a real part of our family again. He's got a great job as a paramedic.

This is Anthony and his girlfriend, Rhonda Jo Applegate. They met one morning when Anthony was answering an emergency call about a choking victim. When he got there, the victim was Rhonda Jo — a beautiful model! Anthony told me and Joey that he had to give her mouth-to-mouth resuscitation! Can you believe it? This is one way she keeps thanking him for saving his life!

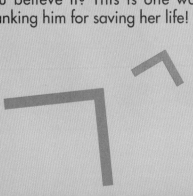

Joey Russo

*T*his is my brother Joey. Everyone says he's a real hunk. Sometimes he even has giggling girls follow him home from school! He's okay, I guess. I mean, he's my brother! Most of the time I don't care *how* cute he is — he can be a real pain!

What's Joey like? Well, how can I say this without sounding mean? Let me put it this way: Out of the three Russo kids, Joey *isn't* the one with the brains in the family!

Listen to this. ... On Joey's birth certificate his name was registered as "B.B. Russo." He slowly became convinced that he and another baby were switched at birth! Dad finally explained to Joey that the B.B. on his birth certificate stood for "Baby Boy" Russo because he and Mom couldn't decide on a name right away.

I do have one thing to say for my brother, though. He, for sure, has a mind of his own. The thing is, his mind is usually one-track! For instance, if the S.A.T.'s tested your knowledge on girls and bikinis instead of math and English, Joey would no doubt have the highest score in the country! No ... in the world!

*H*e may not be the smartest Russo kid, but he's definitely the most athletic. In fact, last year Joey came this close to joining a professional South American baseball team! He declined the position in order to finish high school. I guess my brother isn't really as dumb as he seems.

17

Joey and I have a pretty cool relationship. Sure, we frequently get into fights, but we always make up. I'd do anything for Joey.

Buzz Richman (Grandpa)

My grandfather, Buzz Richman, is not your ordinary, conventional grandpa. Unless, of course, your idea of an ordinary grandfather is someone who double-dates with your 17-year-old brother and spends days at the track and nights at a jazz club. But ever since the day of my fifteenth birthday, when Buzz showed up out of the blue, he's become a big part of our lives. Dad isn't too thrilled about having his ex-wife's father around so much, but I think he doesn't complain because he knows how much Buzz means to Anthony, Joey, and me.

Things I Totally Dig!

*T*alking about this part of my life is easy. I like doing so many different things! Basically, my favorite thing in the world to do is dance. Six and I choreograph routines all the time, and probably the most-excellent thing that has ever happened to me had to do with dancing. It was the time Six and I stayed out all night waiting in line to get front-row tickets to C&C Music Factory's concert. After waiting a zillion hours on line, the ticket office opened up, and … well, to make a long story short — we did not get front-row concert tickets. We were really bummed out! But while Six and I were still outside the ticket office, a limousine pulled up, and guess who stepped out? Robert Clivilles, David Cole, Zelma Davis, and Freedom Williams of C&C Music Factory! Six and I told them that we were their biggest fans and they asked us to prove it. So we got to dance with them to one of their songs! It was totally unbelievable. They're still one of my favorite groups.

I used to spend a lot of time with Vinnie. Sometimes we'd catch a movie, sometimes I'd help him with schoolwork, and sometimes we'd just hang out and talk.

I love hanging out with Six. Of course we spend most of our time together talking, dancing, and shopping, but one of our favorite things to do on a Saturday night (that is, if neither of us has a date!) is rent scary movies. Last Halloween, we rented a bunch and scared ourselves to the max!

*D*ad likes to rent real tear-jerker movies all the time, and it totally drives me crazy. We all watch them together, but I'm always the one who ends up crying! Once before, when Vinnie and I broke up, and Anthony and Rhonda Jo broke up, too, Dad rented *The Way We Were*. Naturally, I cried my eyes out every five minutes.

*B*elieve it or not, I really like to bake. I've cooked for the family lots of times, and I'm proud to say that no one has ever gotten sick from any of my cooking!

*J*oey, on the other hand, doesn't share my enthusiasm about baking. He can't even hold the utensils the right way!

*U*m ... yes, it's true. In addition to cooking and baking, I *love* eating. Here's a shot of me about to pig out!

Six and I are always thinking up new ways to earn money. We've done the baby-sitting thing, the part-time job thing, and once we ran a garage sale and made a bundle. But, I'll get to that later. ...

After putting so much time and money into fixing up my room, there are times that I enjoy just hanging out up there, listening to music or mixing and matching my clothes to make up new outfits.

Best of all, I love to talk on the phone. When Six isn't over (which is rare), we're usually talking on the phone. Sometimes, my mom calls me from Paris. I love hearing about everything she's doing and telling her everything I've been doing. Usually, I write to her (at least once a week) but it's really something special when she calls and I can hear her voice.

25

The Life and Zany Times of The Russo Family

So, you're probably wondering why I said that living in my house is like visiting the *Twilight Zone*. Well, here's why. Do these look like normal people to you? I didn't think so. What would you say if I told you that these Wilson Phillips wannabes are my Dad, Anthony, and Grandpa Buzz???

Okay, okay ... on a more-normal note, here's a quaint little picture of a loving father. (Still don't believe me about the *Twilight Zone?*)

Know when this photo was taken? The day I skipped school and hung out — with my Dad! Things had been getting so hectic at home that my Dad and I practically didn't see each other for days. Dad surprised me by asking me to spend the entire day alone with him. We had a blast: eating at a fancy restaurant, sneaking into movies (we got caught!), and going to a ball game, where we totally pigged out on junk food.

*O*ooh, I remember this day. It was when Dad brought home a *serious* girlfriend — Suzy, I think her name was — to meet us. We were all so nervous that Dad wanted to marry Suzy and that she would become our new mother, we were actually hoping she would be a real loser and Dad would dump her. Anyway, we spent the whole day getting the house beautiful and cooking for Suzy. She was pretty nice, I guess, though Dad ended up breaking up with her a few days later.

*A*ll right. I'm ready to tell you about the time Six got us both thrown in the can. Here's how it happened: We got some stuff together and had a garage sale. We were counting the money we made, when all of a sudden two policemen show up, arrest us for selling stolen goods, and throw us in jail! I'm freaking out and all, and then Six goes and tells me that she *did* steal the stuff we were selling. Right then, I almost passed out! Six told me she needed money to pay for cool new jeans like the ones the popular kids in school wear. Luckily, the jail term won't go on my permanent record or anything, and though I was really, *really* mad at Six, we made up. Her mom and I told her that new clothes wouldn't make her more popular, and that she already had tons of friends anyway.

I remember this day. ... It was the day I was made to feel like the biggest fool in the universe! See, there was this guy — a guitar player in a rock band — who asked me to come watch him play. Six and I asked David, this kid at school, to fix us some fake ID's to get into the club. Well, he did, only the ID's said we were 24 years old! Forget the fact that he made our names Selma and Louise — I knew the bouncer would never believe we were who we were supposed to be.

*W*e got all dressed up anyway, trying to look 24. Once we got to the club, however, the bouncer wouldn't let us in — it was "teen" night, and nobody over 17 was allowed in! Can you believe it? Then we tried to convince the guy that we were really 16, but he didn't believe us. The worst part was, when I told him that I was invited by the guitarist, he told me that *every* girl there was also invited by the guitarist! It was so embarrassing. I felt like a queen-sized dork.

This is from when Six convinced me to run for class president against Eddie Warwick. Eddie didn't waste a second trying to smear my name and my campaign. He told the press that Anthony used to use drugs. Then Six, my campaign manager, told the press that Eddie had had an affair with a teacher, and the mudslinging just blew out of proportion. I ended up losing — but only by 1 percent of the vote. Next year, though, the presidency is mine!

A couple of months ago, Dad's TV-writer friend, Steve, wanted to make a TV sitcom about our family! It was a very weird time for all of us, but the weirdest part of all was when Six and I auditioned for roles on the show. I was sure they'd want me to play "Rosie," the character who was based on me. Boy, did I flip out when Six landed that role! In the end, the show never made it off the ground.

It's really hard trying to have a serious discussion about life with a man dressed in a bunny suit! But this was a really great moment. After I ran away with Vinnie and came back home, Dad and I made up. Ever since then, we've been able to relate to each other better.

I thought Vinnie and I related well to each other, too.

When Vinnie got into a motorcycle accident and was rushed to the hospital, it was the worst night of my life. I sat by his bed for hours, waiting for him to come to. I had all sorts of crazy dreams picturing what life would be like if I spent my life waiting for him to wake up. I was really stressed out. The funniest thing happened that night though. There was this nurse named Doris attending to Vinnie, and she and I started talking and everything, and we really connected. Later, when Vinnie woke up, I found out that Doris is Vinnie's mother!

A few months ago, Six and I got into this really big fight because she thought I was spending all my time with Vinnie and neglecting her. She was right, I guess, but I'm way glad we made up. Nobody could ever take the place of Six!

A Fashion Statement

I've always had a knack for putting together some totally funky, wild outfits. I guess I get that from my mom. She's always been a real free spirit. Whenever Six and I go to the mall or to a second-hand clothing store, we go right to the sales racks and try to find the bargains. We have only one rule — if it's wildly outrageous, it's perfect! Here are a few of my favorite styles.

*N*ot!

So … that's my life. Actually, it's not all that bad. I mean, I have a pretty terrific family (dysfunctional as it may be), and an excellent best friend. What more could a 16-year-old girl ask for? Except maybe a new car, a bigger allowance, no curfew, no boyfriend problems, a credit card in her name …